The Swamp Witch pulled a dusty, black bag out from behind the shelves, all the time muttering to herself about her baby alligators. We watched as she opened the bag. Suddenly, she pointed a long, bony finger at us, and let loose with a crazy laugh.

The hair on my arms stood on end. I knew I had to get out of there! With a scream, I bolted for the door. Michael was right behind me.

A second later we were crashing down the path away from the cottage. Behind us we heard the Swamp Witch's hysterical laugh getting louder. She was following us.

I turned to look for her as I ran. When I turned back around, a scream exploded in my throat. Michael and I couldn't stop ourselves in time.

We ran right into the hanging bones of an ancient skeleton!

The Curse of Blood Swamp

by C.K. Savage

To Ryan and Michael Lauchli—
May you always enjoy the
creepy-crawly things of life.

Published by Worthington Press
7099 Huntley Road, Worthington, Ohio 43085

Copyright ©1990 by Worthington Press

Printed in the United States of America

10 9 8 7 6 5 4 3 2 1

ISBN 0-87406-466-X

Contents

CHAPTER 1
The Swamp Witch Returns

"**R**YAN Patrick Wells! Your cousin Michael's arriving in less than an hour and you still haven't cleaned up your room! Do it now!"

I looked up from the newspaper I was reading to see my mom standing in the doorway to my room. Mothers are always showing up when you're trying to do something important. I got up from my bed and laid the newspaper on my night table.

"All right, Mom. You don't have to have an attack. I was just reading this article about the return of the Swamp Witch. Some guy was missing in the swamp for a week. And when he finally staggered out, he kept mumbling about a horrible old hag who tried to eat him alive!"

"What are you reading? The *National Enquirer?*" She picked up the newspaper and looked at a picture of a figure running through some cypress trees somewhere in the Everglades.

"Is this supposed to be a witch?" she asked. "It looks more like a squished blob."

"Listen, Mom. The police didn't believe the guy who was lost," I continued. "Even though he had the teeth marks on his arm to prove his story. And do you know where he is now?"

"Let me guess. In a spaceship with Elvis?"

I gave Mom a disgusted look. "No," I said. "They locked him up in the state mental hospital. The guy has amnesia and just keeps mumbling about the Swamp Witch. He can't even remember his own name. No one knows who he is!"

"Honestly, Ryan, I don't know why you waste your time reading this garbage when you have homework to do."

"It's not garbage. And I finished my homework yesterday," I told her. "I would have taken it to Rick today, but I had to wait for Michael."

Rick Samuels is my home study advisor. I don't go to a regular school because my parents own an airboat tour business in Big Cypress Swamp, which is part of the Florida Everglades. I drive our airboat to Rick's house once a week. He lives about 20 minutes away.

Mom didn't seem to be as excited about the Swamp Witch as I was. She just pointed to the pile of dirty socks sticking out from under my bed. "Michael will be here any minute," she reminded me. "Finish cleaning your room. And Ryan, don't go filling that boy's head with stories of Swamp Witches and insane people and snakes and bugs. He's from the big city and isn't used to that kind of thing."

He's a *wimp,* I thought. But I didn't say anything. When Mom left, I started grabbing clothes and the stuff that was all over my floor. I put the clothes in the hamper in the bathroom and scooped up papers and magazines and put them on my desk.

The whole time I was cleaning my room, I was thinking about my cousin, Michael. Ever since I could remember, he'd spent a month each summer with us. I guess he's not that bad. We're just interested in completely different things. Even though he's fourteen, just like me, I think he acts like a baby. Being from the city, he's scared of things we have down here in the swamp—things like snakes, bugs, and scorpions. It's pretty fun to scare him with swamp stories and to put harmless critters in his bed at night. I picked up the newspaper story about the legend of the

Swamp Witch. Hmmm, I was getting an idea.

"They're here!" Mom called from the living room.

I stood up slowly and walked into the living room. *I might as well get this over with,* I thought. I looked out the front window toward the boat dock. Who was that big guy with Dad?

I couldn't believe my eyes. It was Michael. He sure had grown up over the winter. Now he was a lot taller than I was.

I walked out to the dock to meet them. After we said hi, I grabbed his two suitcases. "Are you still scared of frogs?" I asked.

"Nah," he answered. "Not since we dissected them in science class."

"Well, how about snakes?" I scared him last year with my pet rat snake, Gertrude.

"That's about enough, Ryan," Dad said. "Let Michael get settled in before you start showing him your pets." Dad had to leave to take some tourists on a trip around the swamp. "See you guys at lunch," he said with a wave as he left in an airboat.

We went back to my room and I set Michael's suitcases in the corner. He didn't look any happier than I did about him being here. "I know you think it's kind of a drag, me coming down here and invading your room, but I can't help it. My parents say I'm still not old enough to stay at home alone when they're gone."

I didn't say anything. I just lay back on my bed and looked at the ceiling.

"Well, how would you like it if your mom and dad sent you up to Chicago for two months?" he asked.

"I don't like the city," I said.

"Fair enough. I don't like the swamp!"

He pulled a battered skateboard out of his duffle bag.

"I guess there aren't any places around here where I can use this," he said as if he was personally insulted about there not being any sidewalks in the Everglades.

"Are you good? On the skateboard, I mean?" I had seen some contests on TV, where guys go flying off into the air and land upside down. It looked really scary.

"I'm okay I guess," he answered. "I've been in a few contests. I got second in one."

"Can you do that thing where you go flying out over the edge of a ramp and hold the skateboard," I asked.

"Not yet, but I'm working on it," he said.

Hmmm, maybe I was wrong about Michael being a wimp. You wouldn't get me near one of those skateboard ramps. For some reason,

I wanted to show him that even though I couldn't skateboard, there was some rough stuff out here in the swamp, too.

"Hey Michael, see those two snakes?" I asked, pointing to two pictures I had taped on my wall. "Those snakes look alike, don't they?"

He looked at the photos and said, "Yeah, I guess so."

I had him now. I'd show him some danger. With a smile, I said, "Well, they're not exactly alike. In fact, knowing which is which is probably a matter of life and death."

"What do you mean?" Michael asked.

I pointed to one picture. "This is a king snake. It's as harmless as a guinea pig. It has red bands bordered by black, then yellow. The color pattern on the other snake is a little different—red, then yellow, then black. But it makes a big difference if one bites you. If it's the second one, the coral snake, it can mean convulsions and heart-attack city."

Michael leaned back and whistled. "I don't know which is worse—poisonous snakes or muggers, like we have in the city."

That remark about muggers reminded me that I had a scary story to try out on my city cousin. "We don't have muggers in the swamp. But we do have something else—a witch!"

"Huh?" he looked at me strangely.

I picked up the newspaper with the story about the Swamp Witch in it. "Have I ever told you about the legend of the Swamp Witch?"

"No. Is it another ghost story?"

"No, it's real. Read this," I said, shoving the article in front of him.

"So?" he said after glancing at the article and the fuzzy photo.

"Don't you get it? The Swamp Witch is back after 30 years and she's living right here in our part of the Everglades. See that tree?" I asked, pointing to the outline of a cypress in the dim background of the picture. "I think I know where that tree is. It's not too far from here."

He rolled his eyes. "Come on, you can't tell anything from this picture. It's so blurry. It's probably a fake, like all those pictures of Bigfoot and the Loch Ness monster."

"It's not a fake. Listen," I said. "Here's the legend. One hundred and fifty years ago, the Swamp Witch was a real person, a witch doctor for the Seminole Indians who lived near here. They say she could charm the swamp creatures. She raised alligators and snakes as pets and used them in her rituals. She practiced healing magic, and everyone trusted her until..." I let my voice trail off dramatically.

"Until what?" Michael asked. I could tell he was starting to get into the story even though he didn't want to.

"Until the chief's son was teasing one of her gators and it attacked him. She couldn't save him. The angry chief ordered every alligator in the swamp to be killed. Then he pronounced the death sentence on the Swamp Witch—she was to walk west into the swamp and never return."

"So she wandered around in the swamp until she died, right?" Michael asked.

"Wrong. First she swore that she would protect her alligator brothers and sisters as long as she lived."

"How long was that?"

"Forever. She didn't die," I whispered. "She perfected her magic and learned the secret of living forever." I tried to make my voice sound eerie to give Michael the full effect. He might be bigger than I am, and he might be a good skateboarder, but I was betting he was still a chicken underneath.

He fidgeted around nervously on the bed. I knew he was thinking about the story because his foot was jiggling a mile a minute.

I leaned a little closer. "From the very beginning, no one has been able to do more than catch a quick glimpse of her before she disappears into the trees. They said she built a chickee—that's a little open-air shack—but no one has ever found that either. Every 30 years she returns. And anybody who's foolish enough to go into her part of the swamp looking for alligators is never heard from again."

"Awww, that's the dumbest thing I've ever heard," Michael said nervously. "What does she do with these people after she catches them?"

"First she cracks her knuckles, and she laughs with her horrible cackling voice. Then she casts spells on them, poisons them, and pickles their bodies to feast on them for the next 30 years. That's how she stays alive. She eats human flesh!"

"Dumb, really dumb," Michael said.

"Yeah? What about those teeth marks on that guy's arm, the one in the article who's now insane from his hideous ordeal in the swamp?"

"You're telling me there's nothing else in that whole swamp that could bite a person?" He turned around to finish unpacking his suitcase. "That's not a bad story. But remind me to tell you about the crazy guy in Chicago who kidnapped a whole family and then held off the police with a machine gun for 48 hours. Now *that's* a scary story. And it's true, too."

When his back was turned, I let out a cackling scream and jumped on him.

"Hee heee heee, I'm the Swamp Witch!"

He yelled and threw me off to one side.

I laughed my head off. "You really believed it. You were scared, admit it. It's only a story," I said through my laughter.

He looked mad. "You just surprised me, that's all. You'd be surprised too if I jumped you when you weren't looking."

I just stood there and cracked my knuckles. Really loud.

CHAPTER 2
Poachers

W E were eating lunch when Dad came back from the tour. He stormed in, exhausted and mad.

"Not one gator!" he bellowed. "Not one lousy gator! The tourists pay good money to see alligators, not flowers and birds and mosquitos!"

"What's going on, Dad? Didn't you go to Beacher's Point? We always see alligators there," I said.

"I went to Beacher's Point. I went to Widow's Lagoon. I even went out of my way and took them to Devil's Cove. But we didn't see one gator."

"Sit down and have some lunch, Terry," my mom told him. "You'll see some this afternoon. You just had a bad morning. Where are the tourists now?"

"Eating lunch out at the picnic table and

snapping pictures like crazy," he answered.

Mom smiled. "See, what did I tell you? They're enjoying themselves. They'll have a good time even if you only see a few alligators this afternoon."

He took a bite of his sandwich. "I guess you're right, Sandy. But it's going to be a bad year if gators are scarce. We'll have to change the name of our business from Gator Watch to Mosquito Patrol."

"I can't believe that you didn't see the alligator colony living at Devil's Cove," I said. "I was by there just yesterday and I saw a bunch of adults and a huge female with a lot of babies. Alligators don't usually leave when their young have just hatched."

"Well, they did leave," answered Dad. "And so have a lot of the others. I don't know what's happening, but gators are disappearing. And if they don't stop disappearing, our business will disappear, too."

The two-way radio crackled just as he swallowed the rest of his milk and slammed the glass down on the table. We don't have a regular phone. We use the radio to talk to other people.

My mother answered. "It's for you, Terry. Darby Yarrow," Mom said.

"Who's Darby Yarrow?" Michael asked.

"He's the head biologist at Big Cypress National Preserve headquarters," Mom said.

"You don't say," my father said into the microphone. "Hides and hatchlings? Well, that would explain why we're not seeing very many."

"What's he talking about?" Michael whispered. "Is something wrong?"

"I don't know," I said, leaning forward to hear better. "But it sounds important."

Dad cleared his throat. "All right, Darby. I'll keep a look out. Yeah, I'll let you know if I see anything suspicious."

He came back to the table. "It seems they've had some trouble with alligator poachers."

"You mean people hunting illegally?" Michael asked.

"Yes. They found a boat in the Gulf of Mexico, over by Everglades City, carrying a huge load of alligator skins and a hold full of baby gators to sell on the black market."

"Did they catch the thieves?" Michael asked.

"No, they just found the boat. But we're supposed to keep our eyes open and let Darby know if we see anything unusual."

"Wow," I said. "We'll go out and scout around right away."

"You'll do no such thing," Mom ordered. "The only scouting you're going to do is to go over to Rick's house and scout out your school assignments for next week."

"Mom, next week is the week I go on the campout with Rick for my science project."

"Oh, that's right. I forgot," Mom said.

"Rick said Michael can go if he wants to," I explained.

"Sure," Michael said. "I'll go."

"Are you sure you're in shape?" I teased him. "I mean, you don't get much exercise in the city, do you? Riding the bus all over the place?"

"You try jumping ramps on a skateboard for six hours and see what kind of shape you're in," he shot back.

"Boys, boys," Mom said. "I'm sure you're both in good shape. But I'm not sure now is such a good time to go on a campout, with the poachers and everything."

"Aw, Mom. The poachers aren't anywhere near here. Dad said they found the boat over near Everglades City. They're probably long gone by now. If I were you, I'd be more worried about the Swamp Witch. She just lives around the corner from us."

"You and your Swamp Witch! I give up," Mom said. "Wash off your plates and get a move on. I want you home by dark."

"Okay, Mom."

"And if you do run into the Swamp Witch," she added, "ask her how her friend the Abominable Snowman likes our Florida weather!"

* * * * *

I love being on the high driver's seat of an airboat. With the prop spinning behind me and the wind in my face, we skimmed across the sawgrass, the long grass that grows in the water. I looked down at Michael in one of the passenger seats. He was holding onto the windshield grab bar so tight that his knuckles were white.

This is a little different from riding on a bus in the big city, I thought. *I'll give you a ride you won't forget.* We hit a strip of shallow water. I yanked the directional stick over to the left, then back to the right, to shake things up a bit. We got going up to 60 miles an hour on a straightaway.

Michael held on, but his face was the color of the gray-green Spanish moss hanging from the big cypress trees. It's not that I dislike my cousin, exactly. I just like to make him squirm.

"Want to drive?" I asked.

"No thanks. I'll just sit down here and enjoy myself."

"It's easier on your stomach if you drive," I told him.

"Nothing's wrong with my stomach," he said.

"Hey, I didn't say there was."

We whizzed past mangrove trees, their bare, red trunks curling and dipping in and out of the water. Dragonflies filled the air and water snakes swam in the thick grasses.

"Mind if we take a quick detour?" I asked.

Michael shook his head. It was probably all he could do to keep from throwing up.

With a flip of the stick, I slowed down and guided the flat-bottom boat onto some solid ground.

"Why'd we stop here?" Michael asked.

"I'm checking out an alligator hole. You did remember to put on bug repellent, didn't you?"

"I'm not stupid," Michael answered.

We got out of the boat and walked quietly to one of the nesting mounds in what we called Gator Tooth Strand. The only sound, except for the buzzing of millions of mosquitos looking for a snack, was the splashes our feet made. We walked for a while. Then I heard that Michael's splashing had stopped. I turned to find Michael staring across the sawgrass prairie toward a strand of gumbo limbo trees. There were hundreds of tall, white birds huddled in the branches.

"What are those?" he asked.

"White ibises. Most city people wouldn't have noticed them," I said. "Maybe there's hope for you yet." We looked at the ibises for a while, until Michael spoke again.

"What's that bird standing over there with the long legs and Pinocchio bill?"

I looked closely to where he pointed and gradually made out a dark brown, speckled form. It was almost impossible to see.

"Awesome eyes, Mike!" I said. "That's a limpkin."

"What is it doing?" he asked.

"Looking for snails to eat," I told him.

We watched the limpkin poke around for a while. Then I said, "Come on, the gators should be right over here.

"Uhh, are you sure it's safe?" Michael asked.

"Yeah. Rick, my teacher, taught me how to approach the nests safely. We'll be careful."

We walked over, but the gators weren't there. The mound was there. And the deep hole carved out of the muck and mud was there. But no gators.

"Maybe they're out walking," Michael said.

"Alligators don't take their babies for walks. They hang around the hole. But even if the mother was off hunting, the babies would still be here. And the mother would have heard us coming a mile away and bellowed a warning."

Suddenly, Michael looked over his shoulder and stared back at the gumbo limbo trees.

"What is it?" I asked. "Another bird?"

"No," he replied slowly. "I thought I saw something moving under those trees. I thought maybe someone was watching us."

A prickly sensation crept up my back and neck. "There's nothing out here but birds and snakes. There aren't even many alligators."

"I don't know," he said with an intense look on his face. "When I first turned around I was sure I saw a face duck behind one of those trees."

"Hey, maybe it was the Swamp Witch," I suggested, hoping a joke would lighten things up.

"Yeah, maybe."

"Let's go look," I said.

But before we could take a step, we heard a wild, wailing call that sounded like a human scream. We both got goose bumps. We watched the limpkin unfold its wings and take off, still crying out its eerie warning. Then, like one large white cloud, the ibises lifted off the tops of the trees.

We both watched the birds fly away. After they had left, the swamp was strangely quiet.

"Uh, listen, we're going to be late to my teacher's house if we don't get going," I said.

"Kinda weird, huh?" he asked as we sloshed back to the airboat. "I still think I saw someone right before the birds took off."

"It was probably your imagination. The limpkin's cries must have set off a chain reaction."

"Maybe you're right," Michael said. Then he was quiet for a while as we walked to the boat. As we got into the airboat, he looked over his shoulder one more time.

"We know that the limpkin scared the ibises," he said. "But what spooked the limpkin in the first place?"

CHAPTER 3
Someone is Watching

WE got to Rick's place a little bit later. It is a small house that blends in really well with the landscape.

"Rick's specialty is wildlife," I explained as we walked up the dock to Rick's. "He works for a university doing research in the swamp. He's great to have for a teacher. He taught me how to find the alligator nests and study them without harming them."

"Maybe Rick can tell us what might have spooked that limpkin," Michael suggested.

"He knows Big Cypress Swamp better than anyone else. If something strange is going on out there, Rick'll know about it," I said.

We knocked on the door. A voice inside told us to come in. There was Rick, sitting at a desk in a corner of the room.

"Hey. Rick. This is my cousin, Michael."

"Nice to meet you, Michael," Rick said.

We talked for a while about the campout, while Michael looked around at all the stuff in Rick's house.

Finally, I asked Rick if he had read the article in the newspaper.

"You mean the one about the guy who went crazy after a week in the swamp?" Rick asked.

"Yeah. Do you think he really saw the Swamp Witch?" I asked.

Rick rubbed his chin. "Well, I think anyone could get pretty scared and have a nervous breakdown if he got lost in the swamp."

"That's not what I mean."

"I'm a scientist," Rick said after a pause. "I deal with facts. But I've lived in this area long enough to see some pretty strange things. Things that can't always be explained by science."

"So you do believe in her!" I said. "Do you think that she discovered the secret of living forever and that she comes back every 30 years and catches people? How about her protecting the alligators in the swamp?"

"Hold it, hold it!" Rick laughed and held up his hands. "I didn't say I believed in her. You seem to know a lot more about her than I do. But anyone who's protecting the animals is on my side, even if she is just a legend."

"Well, have you ever looked for her chickee

hut?" asked Michael. "Just to see if the stories are true?"

Rick shook his head and smiled. "Let's talk about the camping trip instead of this Halloween stuff. I hope you're coming along on our camping trip next week, Michael."

"Sure I am," he answered. "We saw some neat birds today. A limpkin and a whole lot of ibises. Something made the limpkin really freak out, though. It got spooked."

Rick looked at me.

"It wasn't us," I said. "We were quiet and downwind of them, just like you showed me. We waded through the water instead of crashing through the grass. And then Michael thought he saw someone hiding in the trees."

Rick looked serious. "Tell me about it."

Michael concentrated on remembering for a minute. "We were investigating an alligator hole. I had just turned to point out the limpkin I had spotted to Ryan, when it screamed and flew away. I glanced at the tangled mangrove trunks just before the ibises flew off. At first it was only a feeling that someone was watching me. But then I saw what looked kind of like eyes—big yellow eyes, kind of glowing.

"Ahem!" a deep voice cleared his throat behind us.

We all jumped.

A big man wearing a tan ranger uniform was standing just inside the doorway. "I knocked, but you all didn't hear me."

"Hi, Griffin," said Rick.

"Sounds to me like you've seen the Swamp Witch, boy," the man said. "Not many have seen her and lived to tell the story." The man let out a loud, harsh laugh.

"Ryan, Michael, this is Dennis Griffin," said Rick. "He works for the National Park Service."

"What do you do for the Park Service, Mr. Griffin?" Michael asked.

"I take care of gators," he said.

"Mr. Griffin has just been assigned to deal with the poaching problem," Rick explained.

"Speaking of alligators and poaching," Mr. Griffin said, "I'm sorry I walked in on you. But I couldn't help overhearing the story about the empty gator hole. Can you show me exactly where that was on this map?"

He laid out a map of Big Cypress Swamp. I pointed to the alligator nesting site.

"Right there, hmm? Those poacher's sure are daring. Don't your folks run an airboat tour business?" he asked.

"Yes, Gator Watch," I replied.

"So you must know where a lot of the gators live around here," the ranger said. "Not just the obvious places that everyone knows about, but lots of hidden ones, too."

"Yes, I guess so," I answered.

Dennis Griffin dropped into a chair and spread out the map. Red circles marked the areas where alligators had been poached.

"I want you to show me where the gator holes are, Ryan," said Mr. Griffin. "Show me right here on this map."

"Why?" For a second, I just had a funny feeling about this guy. But then I told myself that he was a ranger and that he needed to know about where the gators were."

He looked at me, and I didn't like the look in his eyes. Then he smiled and laughed, like before.

"The reason I need to know, Ryan, is that if I'm going to catch these poachers, I need to know where they might be going. Then we can get there first. The law says we have to catch them in the act of poaching."

"Sure," I said with a shrug. For the next half hour I pointed to places on the map. He circled each place in green as he fired questions at me. He wrote things down in a notebook.

How many gators in that hole? Have the eggs hatched? Are there hatchlings? How many? How many adults? What size?

Finally, Rick looked out the window to the west. "It's getting late," he said. "Your parents will be expecting you boys home for dinner."

"Yep, we'd better be going. Nice to have met you, Mr. Griffin," I said.

"Well, boys," he said, "thank you very much for all this information. This will be very helpful, believe me."

The four of us walked out to the edge of the dock to our airboat.

"I'll see you boys bright and early Monday morning to start our trip," Rick said.

"Trip?" Dennis Griffin said. "I wouldn't advise going on a camping trip while all this trouble with poachers is going on. I'd hate to shoot you by mistake," he paused. "Or see you pickled by the Swamp Witch." He laughed that loud laugh of his.

"Don't worry. We'll be careful," Rick told him.

Mr. Griffin smiled. "Good. You always have to be careful in the swamp, don't you?"

"I don't like that guy Griffin," said Michael as we were pulling away from the dock. "I don't like the way he laughs."

"Neither do I," I agreed.

Michael glanced around at the empty seats. "Uh-oh, we forgot your books."

I hit my forehead with my hand. "I can't believe how stupid I am. I was so anxious to get out of there that I left them on the table. We'll have to go back in the morning."

"Tomorrow," Michael said, "you can teach me how to drive this boat!"

CHAPTER 4
The Pirate's Hook

THE next day was Saturday, our busiest day for giving tours. So we couldn't get over to Rick's in the morning to pick up my stuff. I didn't care about the books so much. What I really needed was my notebook. Everything I wanted to do on our trip was written down in there.

A boatload of tourists had arrived from Everglades City, ready for the all-day tour of Big Cypress National Preserve. Dad took some of the tourists on one airboat and Michael and I took the rest of the group on the other.

Tourists who wanted to see the swamp paid to be transported by motorboat and canoe through the narrow inland waterways. Once they got to our place, the swamp was so thick that the only way in was by airboat or on foot. Plenty of people hiking around in the Everglades had gotten lost and died only a short distance from help. That guy who got out last week was one of the lucky ones. He was only crazy, not dead.

As I steered us across the open grass, I studied our passengers. Four of the five seemed perfectly normal and ordinary. The fifth one was definitely not ordinary.

He was middle-aged. So far, so good. But on the end of one arm was an ugly, metal hook. He was sitting in the front of the boat, writing in a notebook as we cruised through the swamp.

"That Mr. Smith looks like a pirate," Michael whispered to me.

"What did he say he did for a living?" I asked.

"He said he runs a lawn mower repair shop in Orlando," Michael answered.

"I wonder if his arm got caught in a lawn mower?"

"I don't know," Michael said. "And I don't think I'll ask him, either," he added.

After a morning of cruising around and pointing out a lot of things, we stopped to eat our lunches near a mangrove island. Dad had checked the alligator hole that morning, so I knew there'd be something to see. Sure enough, the mother alligator was there, surrounded by a dozen or so squirming babies.

Forgetting about their lunches, the passengers leaned over the rail and did some serious gator gawking. The mother gator was thrashing her tail around, digging deeper into the mud. The babies played on a wide log.

Mr. Smith took notes with his good hand while his hook held a clipboard. He was still taking notes by our third alligator stop.

"Have you noticed that he doesn't take notes on any of the bird stops?" Michael whispered to me as we looked at another alligator hole, one that I'd mentioned the day before to Dennis Griffin.

"Huh? Sorry, I wasn't listening," I told him. "Look over there. Does anything look strange to you?" I pointed to the muddy bank of the water hole. Three gators were lounging on the shore.

Michael looked where I was pointing, but shook his head.

"See that place where the grass is all flattened out? It looks like something was dragged out of there."

"Is that where the gators slide into the water?" Michael wondered.

"No," I pointed to the other side of the bank, where the mud was carved in smooth, hollowed-out trenches. "That's what it looks like when they slide in. That area over there looks like it was trampled by people."

"Do you think the poachers have been here?" Michael asked. "Are any alligators missing?"

"It's kind of hard to tell." I looked over to see Mr. Smith staring at us. "We'll have to come back to investigate later," I whispered to Michael.

"Yeah," he answered, "when we don't have so much of an audience."

Right then, I realized I had started to change my mind about Michael. He didn't seem like a wimp at all anymore. Maybe he never was one to begin with. I just figured that since he was from the city, he was squeamish about things. Now that we were doing some stuff together, he was starting to seem like a regular guy. And I was glad I didn't have to worry about this poaching stuff by myself.

When we finally dropped the passengers off back at their boat, it was only about an hour from sunset. We grabbed a quick bite at home, then got the airboat out again to go over to Rick's to get my stuff.

"You boys be careful," Mom said as we left. "Be back before dark."

"It will only take us a little while," I told her. "We just need to zip over to Rick's house and pick up my books."

We were planning to stop by the last gator hole to check it out on the way over to Rick's. Michael and I didn't speak as we brought the airboat up to full power and flew across the grass. Not because we had nothing to say. Twilight is the worst time to be out in the Everglades. The air is practically solid mosquitos. And if you open your mouth, you get bugs in your teeth. It's as simple as that.

We put on goggles to keep the bugs out of our eyes. The sun was just setting red against the horizon when we spotted the alligator hole. We idled up, then cut the engine. Hip boots on, we waded quietly through the grass to the edge of the hole.

It was quiet, almost too quiet. The baby gators were all snuggled in a heap in the center of the nest, but the adults weren't around. There had been no bellow of warning when we slogged up to the hole.

"I saw the mother and two other adults when we were here today," I said to Michael. I sloshed my way over to the sandy grass area.

"Someone has definitely been here since then," I whispered. I pointed to a large black-ish-red stain on the grass.

"Is that blood?" Michael asked.

"It sure looks like it. The poachers must

have stolen more alligators since we were here earlier this afternoon."

Michael looked around warily. "Do you think any gators are still around? Where's the mother now?"

"I don't know. Maybe the poachers killed her."

We followed the trail made by the dragging of dead alligators. Smears of blood dotted the path. On the other side of a clump of moss-draped trees, the trail led to an open prairie. I pointed to a big open place that had been flattened.

"We missed this because we parked on the other side," I said. "There's definitely been an airboat here."

"Darn!" I kicked at the ground. "Let's go back and count the babies."

The sun was almost down, so we ran as quickly as we could back to the hole, not trying to be quiet.

"What are we going to do if the poachers took the mother, too?" I wondered out loud. "The babies can't survive on their own. And we can't leave them here. The poachers might come back for them. Maybe Dad will know what to do."

At the gator hole, we leaned far out to count the foot-long babies. I knew there were at least

20 the week before, and at least a dozen today. But tonight I could only count six.

I tried to poke around in the grassy nest to see if there were any more babies hidden down there. Only the yelping distress calls of the baby alligators broke the silence.

"I think we should go," Michael suggested. "It's getting pretty dark. Plus, I have that funny feeling that we're being watched again."

"You're right," I said. "We'll have to hurry if we're going to make it to Rick's house tonight."

Suddenly, not more than 10 feet away from us, the mother alligator opened her wide jaws in an angry bellow. Her golden eyes flashed in the fading light.

We both screamed. "Let's get out of here!" I yelled. Giving our boots a mighty yank to pull them out of the slime, we tore off as fast as we could to get away from the angry gator. Down the path we ran, with the hanging moss slapping at our faces. The mother alligator was hot on our heels. Alligators, especially mad ones, move faster than people in the swamp.

"Climb!" I shouted as we reached the cypress trees.

The mother gator's snapping jaws came together on the heel of my rubber boot just as

I hauled myself up into the nearest tree. I wiggled my foot free and hung onto the crooked trunk, dangling one tennis shoe. My boot fell down to the ground. The mother alligator chomped on my boot and hissed at us.

"Will she ever go away?" Michael said from the next tree.

"Sooner or later, she'll have to go check on her babies," I said. "But I don't think we're going to get to Rick's tonight."

We sat in our trees, looking down at the alligator as she devoured my boot. Suddenly, Michael pointed across the sawgrass to the deepest part of the swamp. "Do you see that light?"

I nodded. The light flickered in and out among the trees. Sometimes it disappeared for a while and then appeared again in a different place.

"What do you think it is?" Michael whispered.

"It could be the poachers," I answered, "or..."

"You don't think it's the Swamp Witch, do you?" he asked anxiously.

"Who knows?" I asked.

"Shh!" said Michael. "Do you hear that?"

We heard a low humming sound. It was faint

at first, but it got louder and louder until it almost drowned out the sounds of the insects. I looked down at the mother alligator, and I almost thought she was listening to the sound, too. Then she flipped her tail around and scooted away.

I breathed a big sigh of relief. But looking back across the swamp where the light had been, I saw that it had turned red, bathing the distant trees in an eerie glow. Suddenly the humming stopped.

And the light went out.

CHAPTER 5
Blood on the Grass

THE first thing we needed to do was talk to my parents. When we got home, things were pretty crazy.

"Darby Yarrow called again," Dad explained. "He wants your mother and me to go down to a special emergency meeting about the alligator poaching at the Game and Fish Department."

"When?" I asked.

"Tomorrow morning. I already talked to Rick Samuels and he said it was all right if you boys left on your trip a day early. He expects you there at dawn tomorrow."

"That's great! Come on, Michael. We have to go get our stuff ready."

We packed our supplies and backpacks and got a little bit of sleep. But we were both pretty excited about the trip in the swamp with Rick, so we didn't sleep too well. The next morning was pretty crazy, with us going camping and Mom and Dad going to the emergency seminar.

"Now, be careful on your trip," Dad said. "Do everything Rick tells you. Here are the radio call numbers of the park authorities and the doctors, in case there's an emergency."

"Are you sure you feel all right about us taking our radios in to have them serviced?" Mom asked.

"Don't worry, Mom, we're going to be with Rick for the whole week. We'll be fine."

"I know you'll be fine," she said, messing up my hair. "I guess mothers just can't quit acting like mothers—even when their babies grow up."

I made a face at Michael. "Babies! Give me a break!"

We waved until they were out of sight. Then we loaded our stuff into the airboat and hopped in, just as the light of dawn began creeping over the trees. I realized suddenly that in our excitement about the trip, Michael and I forgot to mention what happened at the gator hole. We decided to tell Mom and Dad all about it as soon as we got back.

We both watched the trees carefully as we cruised to Rick's. And I knew Michael was listening as hard as I was for that low hum, the one that seemed to have frightened the mother alligator. I couldn't wait to ask Rick what he thought about it.

But there was something wrong when we got to Rick's. Something very wrong.

"I wonder why Rick's door is open?" I asked as we tied the airboat to the dock.

"Maybe he's loading?" Michael suggested.

"But where's the canoe?" I asked, looking around. "We're supposed to do the first part of our trip by canoe."

"Rick!" I called out anxiously as I jogged up the dock. "Rick!"

But my voice was swallowed up by the silence of the morning. Carefully, we pushed the door open the rest of the way and peeked inside.

"Oh no!" I cried.

The hut was a disaster. Clothes, books, papers, even the pots and pans were thrown everywhere. But Rick was nowhere to be found. I looked at Michael and knew that he was thinking what I was thinking.

"Who would do something like this?" he asked. "Rick is just a teacher and scientist. He doesn't have anything valuable."

"No," I answered slowly. "But maybe he *knew* something valuable."

We searched the ransacked room, trying not

to disturb anything that might be a clue. We looked behind everything and inside everything. But we couldn't find anything at all that gave us any clue about what had happened to Rick.

I flopped down in a chair. "It's no use," I said. "Whoever it was must have surprised him."

Michael hit the table with his fist. "If we had only gotten here earlier, we might have been able to stop them!"

"We didn't know," I said.

"Maybe not, but what are we going to do now?" He picked up my notebook that was lying on the table. Tossing it over to me, he said, "Here's your list of things to do on the camping trip—a lot of good it'll do us now."

I absent-mindedly opened the notebook. There, written on the first page, was a message that jumped out at me.

"Michael, listen to this! Rick must have scribbled a note before they got him. It says, 'Stop them. Find the Swamp Witch.'"

"What? Let me see!"

I passed the notebook to him. "But what does it mean?" he asked.

"It means we have to call the Park Police— right away! Come on, Rick's radio is out on the back porch."

We leaped over the mess on the floor and burst through the door to the back porch at the same time. My heart was pounding as I reached for the microphone.

"This is Ryan Wells," I shouted into the mike. "Come in. This is an emergency. Come in."

But there was no sound, not even static.

Michael reached behind the table and picked up the battery pack. It was smashed. He held out the cord to the receiver. It was cut into about 10 pieces.

"We can rig another battery," I said, reaching into the storage cabinet for more wire. "And I think I can splice the cord back together."

"We're out of luck, unless you can build another one of those," Michael said, pointing out into the yard. "They trashed the antenna, too."

I ran down the back steps and looked at the pile of broken antenna pieces at my feet. "These guys mean business," I said.

We walked back inside and sat down.

"Maybe we'd better get out of here," Michael said. "What if they come back?"

"But where do we go? It might not be safe back at our house either," I told him. "I think we have to do what Rick said. We have to try to find the Swamp Witch."

"Ryan, the Swamp Witch is just a story," Michael said. "It's fun for around the campfire. But a story won't help us find Rick."

"I know that. But maybe the words, 'Swamp Witch' are like a code or something. Maybe they're a clue to tell us where to look."

I looked at him, feeling the fear build in my chest. "We have to try. There's no one else who can help him now. Look, maybe Rick wrote 'Swamp Witch' because he thought they were going to take him out to the Black Swamp, where the witch is supposed to live. Maybe it's something like that."

"Maybe. But how do we know? We could wander around out there for years and never find him."

We walked outside and down to the edge of the water.

"There has to be a clue," I said. "Think! They took his canoe, so they must have followed one of the inland creeks. The Black Swamp is where we saw that light last night. Maybe that was the light on their boat."

"Uh-oh, Ryan. Look at this," Michael said.

He pointed to a spot near the canoe launch where a lot of muddy footprints were all over the ground. I knelt down and touched a wet, dark spot on the grass.

"It looks like Rick put up a fight," I said. "It's blood."

We stared at the blades of blood-soaked grass near the launch site. "At least we know he was alive," Michael said finally. "They wouldn't have taken him if he wasn't alive, would they?"

"Probably not," I answered.

"Hey, look at this," Michael said. Half sticking out of the water was a dead baby alligator. I brushed the sand off of it and laid it down on the ground. There was a piece of a flower stuck in its claw. I stared at the poor thing for a minute or two. Then something caught my eye and jogged my memory.

"Michael! This is a piece of a worm vine orchid!"

"Uh, what does that mean?" he asked.

"It means this alligator was definitely taken from the Black Swamp. I know it was. Rick showed me this kind of flower just last week. It only grows in the most hidden section of the Everglades. This has to be a clue."

"But how are we going to get there?" Michael asked. "They took the canoe, and we can't follow them in the airboat. It's too big."

"Wait a minute. I know something that will help us—something the kidnappers didn't know about!"

CHAPTER 6
Hanging Harry

"RICK has been carving a dugout canoe from the trunk of a cypress tree," I explained. "Just like the Indians used to do. And he showed me where he's keeping it."

I led Michael out to a clump of pines behind the hut. We dragged the heavy, rough-looking canoe out to the water's edge. Luckily, the paddles were inside it.

"I guess if it's good enough for the Indians, it's good enough for us," Michael said.

"Before we go, we'd better leave a message here for my parents about where we're going and what we're doing. They won't be back for almost a week, but I can't think of anything else to do. Even if we went back to our house, we couldn't radio for help because Dad took the radio equipment with him."

"Besides, it could be dangerous," Michael added.

We taped a note to the door of Rick's hut and set off on our trip. We paddled toward the Black Swamp the whole morning. Then we stopped to rest and eat lunch. It was really getting hot, and paddling that dugout canoe was hard work. We pressed on through the steamy afternoon. Just as it was beginning to get dark—and as the bugs were starting to come out—we spotted Rick's canoe pulled up on the bank and covered with a few branches.

We paddled up to it as quietly as we could and looked around.

"Footprints," Michael said. "They look pretty old, though."

We decided to go hide our canoe, in case they came back that way. We didn't want them to know we were after them. It was dark by the time we hid our canoe a quarter-mile downstream and hiked back to the site.

"We might as as well make camp here," I said. "We can't follow their trail in the dark."

We built a small fire and decided to take turns keeping watch. But we were too exhausted from the paddling. We both fell asleep. Mixed in with my dreams were the sounds of the swamp all around me.

Sometime in the middle of the night, I was startled out of my sleep by a hideous sound. It was a horrible, high-pitched cackle!

Michael and I jerked to our knees and tried to get out of our sleeping bags. But we were all tangled up from rolling around while we were asleep.

"W-w-what was that?" Michael stuttered.

"I think it came from over there," I said, pointing into the trees.

But then we heard the cackle from a different direction.

"Look! Over there!" Michael screamed.

Two yellowish eyes peered out at us from behind a tree. We heard the cackle again. I reached for a rock and threw it as hard as I could at the glowing eyes.

When the rock hit the tree, a large bird screeched and flew away into the night. The eyes were gone. We breathed a little easier.

I laughed. "That was kind of spooky," I said. "I thought that bird was...you know...the Swamp Witch."

"Yeah," Michael answered in a shaky voice. "Your eyes can play tricks on you here in the swamp."

"Let's try to get some sleep," I said.

But as soon as we lay back down, we heard the horrible cackle again, and a dark figure stepped into the fading light of our campfire.

"Ah-ha-ha-ha-ha-ha-ha-ha!"

"Arrgghh!" Michael and I screamed.

"Don't hurt us! Please!" I cried. "We don't mean any harm!"

We tried to scoot away from the figure, but we couldn't move. The creature, or whatever it was, was standing on the ends of our sleeping bags! Michael and I were babbling hysterically.

"Please don't do anything to us. Don't eat us! We're only trying to find our friend, Rick Samuels. He—"

"Friends of Rick's, eh?" she asked in a screechy voice.

"H-h-huh? You know Rick?" I asked. What was going on?

"Well," she answered, "let's just say I've heard of him and what he's doing to help the animals of the swamp."

The creature stepped closer to the fire and we could see more of it. It was definitely a woman, but she didn't seem old, like I pictured the Swamp Witch. She was wearing a cloak with a hood, and she was barefoot.

"Y-y-y-yes," Michael told her. "Rick sent us to find you. We think he has been kidnapped by some poachers. He left a note saying we should find you—if you're the Swamp Witch, that is."

She cackled again and said, "That's what some people call me."

We just stared, not knowing what to think.

"You boys are a little nervous, aren't you?"

"No! We're not nervous!" screeched Michael. "Well, I mean, it's just that, you know, we thought you were, umm..."

"Dead?" she shrieked. Then with a chuckle, she added, "Do I look dead to you?"

Not dead, exactly, I thought. *But weird. Definitely creepy and weird!*

"I'll tell you what," she said in a normal voice. "If you want to know the whole story, you'll have to come to my cabin." She looked around at our campsite. "You don't even have any mosquito netting. If you're not careful, you'll be eaten alive..."

"What?" we said together.

"By the mosquitos!" she added, with a grin.

We hesitated.

"Come on, boys. If I was going to do anything to you, wouldn't I have done it already? You'll be much more comfortable in my hut. And shake out those sleeping bags," she added. "I don't want any scorpions or snakes as house guests."

We gathered up our stuff and started to follow her through the swamp. I don't know why we went with her. Maybe it was because she knew Rick. Or maybe it was because she had put a spell on us.

In the light of the moon, I had a chance to study her as we walked. She wore the cloak and a long-sleeved blouse. Her long skirt was made of colored cloth strips. She wore her black hair in a long braid in the style of the Seminole Indians, the tribe that had lived in the Everglades for centuries.

She didn't speak as she led us through the overgrown swamp. I don't remember the path she took, but she had no trouble following it in her bare feet. She could really move fast, and sometimes we had trouble keeping up with her. When I looked back from where we had come, the leaves and moss seemed to have grown up to cover our tracks. It was like the swamp was swallowing us up.

I had no sense of time. What could have been five minutes or an hour later, we came out into a clearing.

"Home sweet home," she said, waving her arm at a ramshackle cottage.

A single candle burned in the cobweb-covered window. I shivered again and I knew it wasn't from the cold. It was from seeing the long row of barrels lined up along the side of the cottage. The barrels were big enough for a man to fit in.

The place looked centuries old, just like the legend said. The rotting cypress stilts covered with cracked deer skins were topped with an ancient roof of palm leaves.

"Sit down, sit down," she said, pointing to some old chairs along the wall. I felt as if I was moving slowly, like in a dream. I wondered if this was what it was like to be under a witch's spell.

The Swamp Witch lit two oil lamps and walked to a small iron stove to stir a large bubbling kettle. Michael and I looked at each other as she shook some powder into the pot.

Michael silently mouthed the word *poison.*

"Hungry?" she asked, stirring the stuff with a long wooden spoon.

I shook my head. But I *was* hungry, really hungry, and the stuff did smell great. "What...what is it?" I asked.

She threw back her head and laughed. Then she opened her eyes so wide I thought they would pop out of her head. She leaned toward me until her face was only inches from mine.

"Rabbit stew," she replied. "I make the best rabbit stew in the Everglades."

She ladled out three steaming bowls of stew and put them on the table. Out of another small pot she poured us cups of black tea that smelled like licorice.

Michael and I both waited for her to take the first bite before we tasted ours.

I studied the room as we ate. It was clean, not a cobweb to be seen. Besides the chairs and table, there was a basin with water and a long set of shelves filled with bottles. I could see small creatures in the bottles. I wasn't sure I wanted to know what they were.

"Let me introduce myself," the witch said, after a time. "My name is Roselyn. I'm a scientist for the Park Service. Alligators are my specialty. And these," she said, pointing to the bottles, "are some of my specimens."

"Huh?" I said under my breath. It just didn't make sense that she was a scientist. "But why do you live like this? What's with the Swamp Witch routine?"

She smiled. "I thought you were wondering that. The thing is, I need to be alone to do my work. If people think there's a witch in here, they won't come snooping around, will they? Besides," she added with a cackle, "I sort of like being a witch. It's fun!"

"Well, you're pretty good at it," said Michael.

"Is that how you know who Rick is?" I asked. "Because you both work for the Park Service?"

"I guess you could say that," she answered. "We both want to protect the alligators. I feel like it's my mission in life to protect them from evil people who want to kill them."

When she talked about people killing alligators, she got a scary look in her eyes. It made me feel like I wouldn't want to run into Roselyn with an alligator skin in my hand. I didn't know what she would do to anybody she caught. But I had a feeling it wouldn't be very pleasant.

I started to feel a little less nervous about her. But there was still a lot that was weird. I just didn't know what to believe. It was so strange watching her and listening to her talk. She looked as if she had just stepped out of an ancient Seminole village. But she talked like a normal, modern person who had gone to college.

"So tell me everything that's happened," she said.

As the swamp began to get lighter, we told her about finding Rick's place all torn up, finding the note, and following the clues. We told her about Mr. Smith, the guy with the hook, and Dennis Griffin, the new ranger. And we told her about finding the alligator hole that was robbed.

"Very good," she said. "You boys did the right thing coming to me. Together we'll save Rick and capture the poachers."

"We don't know how much time we have," Michael told her. "They could be a whole day ahead of us already."

"They could be. But they don't know the swamp the way I do," Roselyn said. She began to pace. Her hair came loose.

"We'll find them," she vowed. "I know we will. The trouble is, the law says you have to catch them in the act and hold them until the authorities arrive."

She was getting really intense. I started to feel a little uneasy again. Sometimes I thought she just might be a little crazy, like maybe she had spent too much time alone out in the swamp.

"How are we going to do that?" I asked, backing away from the strange gleam in her eye.

She cracked her knuckles and said with a loud cackle, "I've got just the thing!"

She pulled a dusty, black bag out from behind the shelves, all the time muttering to herself about her baby alligators. We watched as she opened the bag. Suddenly, she pointed a long, bony finger at us, and let loose with a crazy laugh.

The hair on my arms stood on end. I had to get out of there! With a scream, I bolted for the door. Michael was right behind me.

A second later we were crashing down the path away from the cottage, screaming at the top of our lungs. Behind us we heard the Swamp Witch's laugh getting louder and more hair-raising. She was following us.

I turned to look for her and kept running. When I turned back around, a scream exploded in my throat. Michael and I couldn't stop ourselves in time.

We ran right into the hanging bones of an ancient skeleton!

Our screams disappeared into the deep swamp. We turned to run the other way, but there was Roselyn, black bag in hand, coming toward us.

"I see you found my friend, Harry," she said. "Harry has seen better days, I'm afraid. I keep him around to scare off unwanted visitors."

I gulped. Harry hadn't been anyone's friend for a long, long time. His bony fingers seemed to reach out to me as I backed away from the witch. Green-gray moss and purple lichen covered the decaying bones, holding them together, letting them sway in the breeze.

As I watched, a fat, green swamp slug oozed its way slowly out of the skeleton's eye.

Right in front of us, the Swamp Witch once again reached deep into her black bag.

Her laughter echoed in my ears. I closed my eyes. I knew whatever she pulled out of that bag would mean the end of us.

CHAPTER 7
The Smell of Death

"SO, do you boys think this rope will hold the poachers? It's pretty old, but I think it's sturdy enough," Roselyn said, pulling a noose out of the bag.

Slowly I opened my eyes, just a crack. The Swamp Witch smiled a strange smile.

"A rope?" I choked out. "You've got a rope in that bag?"

"Well, what else would we use to keep the poachers from getting away? Perhaps a secret potion? Or a magic spell? By the way, I hope I didn't frighten you back there. Sometimes I just get carried away when I think about people hurting my alligators. I can feel their pain when they're murdered. I can feel the sadness of the babies when their mothers are taken away from them."

"Uh, well," Michael said, "hey, no problem. We weren't scared, were we, Ryan?"

"Oh... no!" I sputtered.

Michael shot me a quick glance and rolled his eyes. The look said, *This woman's crazy. We'd better keep an eye on her!*

"No more fooling around," Roselyn said, turning quickly and trotting back to the cabin. "We have work to do!"

We took one last look at Harry's face, shimmering with a trail of slug slime. Then we followed Roselyn.

"Crazy or not," I whispered to Michael. "She's our only hope to find Rick and catch the poachers."

He nodded. "I guess we don't have much choice. We'll have to trust her. But we've got to be careful. She's totally weird."

In less than an hour, we had packed our stuff and were on our way. We followed the trail back to where Rick's canoe was hidden and started from there. Roselyn said there were three men.

"Three sets of footprints? That means Rick isn't dead," I said.

"Not yet," added the Swamp Witch.

As we walked I had a chance to study her. It was impossible to tell how old she was. She used a walking stick, but it was more for jabbing and poking ahead of her than to lean on. Her black hair was streaked with gray, but she didn't have any wrinkles on her face. Her voice sounded old, but we practically had to run to keep up with her.

The Swamp Witch's bare feet made no sound as she picked her way through the swamp. At one rest stop, I finally had the nerve to ask, "What are all the barrels out behind your house, Roselyn?"

"They're filled with drinking water," she explained. "I collect rainwater to drink and use for washing. Would you drink out of the swamp?" she asked sarcastically.

I must have looked relieved. She smiled and added, "Of course, there's formaldehyde in two of them—for preserving specimens."

A short time after that, we came upon a meadow of sawgrass. In the center was the large rounded dome of an alligator nest. It was the highest land for miles around.

As we got closer, we saw the wide pool surrounding the nest. It was at least 25 feet across.

Roselyn stood on the edge of the pool, listening and watching. "This is one of my favorite spots," she told us. Several alligator families live here."

"Where are they now?" I asked. A tiny snake slipping under a morning glory blossom was the only movement.

"I smell death," Roselyn said. She started running. We followed her to the other side of the gator pool.

Black clouds rolled across the sky as we stared at the raided nest. There were no young alligators left, only broken eggs and the ripped-apart nest.

"Only another week and the rest would have hatched," she wailed.

Thunder rumbled in the distance as we watched a transformation come over her. Gone was the scientist. In her place was the Swamp Witch. The more the storm built around us, the angrier she became. She raised her stick in the air as lightning flashed.

Cursing the poachers, she danced around the deserted swamp, begging the lightning to strike the evil men who had destroyed the alligators. Michael and I moved away from her, inching backward into the tall grass.

Suddenly we tripped against something soft and wet. Michael stumbled and fell.

"Aaaggh!" he yelled, jumping up quickly. Beneath our feet were the bloody carcasses of at least six adult alligators. They had been skinned, their teeth pulled out, and their tails stripped for the meat.

I almost got sick. The stew we had eaten for breakfast threatened to come up.

"Roselyn," I said in a weak voice that didn't even sound like mine, "you'd better see this."

She came over and stood by us as the rain started to fall. It washed away most of the slaughter in rivers of red. Her quiet seemed more frightening than her rage.

"Come on," Roselyn said. "I know a place where we can keep our equipment dry. We can scout around for clues, get some sleep, and then move again at night. We'll find them then. I guarantee we'll find them!"

I took one last look at the pile of dead alligators and we left. "I'm sure glad she's on our side," I whispered to Michael as we slogged along after her to the trees.

"You're not kidding," Michael agreed.

We'd hidden our gear under a shelter. Roselyn explained that she had built it earlier to observe alligator families. "How close do you think the poachers are?" Michael asked.

"I think they're very close," she said. "So close that they may even know we're here."

I glanced around, looking for any sign that we were being watched.

"I have an idea," she said in a low voice as thunder rumbled in the distance. "We'll walk back toward my cabin. Maybe we can convince them that we've given up. Then we'll double back, get our gear, and sneak up on them."

It was almost dark when we finally hiked back to the shelter. Exhausted and wet, we unrolled our sleeping bags and ate a cold meal of beef jerky and crackers. We washed it down with rainwater gathered in the upturned leaves of the saw palmetto.

The whole time we were eating, Roselyn paced back and forth in front of the shelter, slapping her walking stick on the ground.

"We'd better get a few hours of sleep," she said. "We'll move again at moonrise."

Michael and I strung the net hammocks that Roselyn had loaned us between two trees. We took off our wet boots and hung them inside the shelter. Michael got into his sleeping bag and sat down on his hammock before swinging his legs up to lie down.

I was just about to do the same when SMACK! Roselyn's walking stick crashed down on my sleeping bag, just missing my foot.

"Move!" she said in a low voice filled with tension.

You can believe I didn't waste any time backing away from her as she slammed her stick down again onto my sleeping bag.

"What is it? What's wrong?" I cried, standing up.

"This is what's wrong, Ryan." She picked

up the end of my sleeping bag and shook it. Out fell a giant scorpion, its tail still twitching in death. It was at least eight inches long. I started to shake uncontrollably to think that one sting, and it could have been my dead body being shaken out onto the ground.

CHAPTER 8
Lost in the Black Swamp

IT must have been close to midnight when I finally dozed off. When the sun was just starting to come up, Michael shook me awake. "She's gone," he said. "Roselyn is gone."

I sat up, rubbing my eyes. "What do you mean, gone?"

"Gone, as in she's not here. Our gear's gone, too."

Sure enough, when I looked at the pegs where we had hung our backpacks, they were empty. Where Roselyn had been sleeping, there was only bare ground.

"At least she left us our boots and sleeping bags," I said. "But why would she take our packs?" I asked.

"I don't know. Do you know where we are?" he asked. "Can you find your way out of here?"

"Yeah, I guess so. My compass is...in my pack," I said. It was like reality slapping me in the face, making me wide awake. "Oh, no! She wouldn't really go off and leave us, would she?"

"Maybe she's really in cahoots with the poachers?" Michael suggested.

"No, I don't think that's it," I answered. "But I sure can't figure her out."

"What are we going to do?" Michael worried out loud. "We came out here looking for Rick, and we'll be lucky if we get out of this swamp ourselves. Boy, I wish I was home now."

That was the first time I had heard Michael say anything about home since the day he arrived. There had been so much excitement from the beginning of his stay.

"Well, we can't sit here and wait for the poachers to find us. We'd better pick out some landmarks and try to follow the poachers' trail. Along the way I'll try to spot some cattail plants for breakfast. They taste a little like potatoes."

"See if you can spot some wild orange juice while you're at it," he joked.

"And some wild bacon and eggs..."

"And a wild English muffin..."

"Maybe I can find the rare, sweet roll bush," I added.

We clowned around to keep our minds off the tough spot we were in. A whole lot of hard questions ran through my mind. What if we couldn't find Rick? What if we did find Rick and he was dead? What if we were hopelessly lost ourselves? What if my parents didn't get home in time to find our note at Rick's house and come looking for us?

I didn't have any answers to these questions. It was easier to think about breakfast.

The swamp closed in around us as we followed the crushed grass and blood-stained trail of the poachers. But the rain had washed away most of the evidence and the trail was hard to follow. As time went on, we had to look for signs that they had passed, such as broken twigs, trampled grass, or bits of alligator eggshell.

It was terrible walking, with the mosquitos and other bugs, the wet, the heat, and everything else.

"How long have we been walking?" Michael asked after a while.

"Three hours," I said, looking at my watch.

"I wonder if we're any closer to them. We haven't seen a sign in a while. And I'm still waiting for my wild potatoes."

We sat down on a fallen log. It was obvious we didn't have a clue about where we were or where the poachers were.

"Notice how the sounds of the swamp get

so much louder as soon as we stop walking?" Michael asked.

I wrung out the cuffs of my jeans and poured the water out of my boots. "Yeah, we must sound pretty noisy to a swamp creature."

"You're beginning to look like a swamp creature yourself," Michael said.

I looked at his dirty, sweaty face, the steam rising into the air from his clothes, and the sand and grass and muck clinging to his pants. "If I look anything like you," I told him, "all I can say is *ribbet!*"

"What I wouldn't give for a snow cone right now," Michael said.

"You know it," I agreed. "I could drink a two-liter bottle of—"

CRACK! CRACK!

The swamp echoed with the sound of gunshots. They seemed to come from all around us. We ran toward where we thought the shots had come from, but it was hard to tell. We ran for what seemed like hours. At one point we stopped on the edge of a pond covered with water lettuce, floating ferns, and duckweed.

"Eat this stuff," I told Michael, handing him some of the water lettuce. "It's bitter, but it's better than starving."

We couldn't stay there long because two big

gators swam up near us, with only their eyes and noses visible above the water. It was almost dark again when we finally stopped to rest on a log.

"Haven't we been here before?" Michael asked.

"Maybe we have," I answered. "I don't know."

"What do you mean you don't know?" Michael shot back. "I thought you were Mr. Wilderness Camper. Now you're telling me we're lost. That's just great!"

"I usually have a compass and a map, Mr. Skateboard!"

"Now you tell me!" Michael yelled.

He gave me a shove and I fell back off the log. I hooked his leg so he fell, too. We were about to start fighting when I saw it. I yelled to Michael, but I was too late.

He let out a scream of pain and started jumping and shaking his hand. Wrapped around his wrist, its fangs sunk into his hand, was a three-foot long, red, yellow, and black snake.

"Slam it against the tree, Michael," I shouted. "That's a coral snake. Kill it before it shoots any more poison into you!"

But he was jumping around howling in pain. I grabbed his arm and slammed his hand against a tree. Once, twice, three times I bashed the snake's head. Blood mingled with snake guts on the tree bark. Finally, the coral snake dropped off his arm, dead.

I half dragged, half carried Michael back to the lettuce pond and plunged his hand under water. I tore a strip off my shirt and tied it around his arm, just above the bite, to try to keep the poison from getting to his body and heart.

"Michael!" I shouted. "Michael, pay attention!" His eyelids were already drooping a little.

"I'm fine, Ryan," he answered. "Just let me rest here until I catch my breath."

"No! You can't rest. We don't have much time—a few hours at most. You feel fine now, but pretty soon the poison will make you weak. We have to get you out of the swamp."

I dragged him to his feet. "You need anti-venin medicine. Do you hear me?" I shouted.

"I hear...you," he said, jerking his hand away and shaking it again, as if the snake was still there. He looked like he was starting to go into shock.

I looked up and saw the sun inching down toward the western horizon. "We're going to walk west," I told him. I put his arm around my shoulder and started walking.

I don't know how I had the strength to keep going. All I knew was that if I failed to keep him moving, the poison would probably kill him. I kept him talking about anything and everything, just to keep him conscious. I asked him to describe his bedroom at home, every inch of it. A couple of times he started laughing hysterically. Rick had taught me that giddiness was one of the signs that the poison was spreading.

It wasn't easy walking. Michael's breathing became more and more difficult. His legs wobbled and his heart was beating a mile a minute. After a while, he stopped talking, just grunting answers to my questions.

I was determined not to go in a circle this time. As we struggled along, I kept my eyes focused on the setting sun. And as darkness fell, my eyes kept concentrating on the last golden glow. *There goes the sun,* I thought. *That's our last chance.*

But, incredibly, the glow on the horizon didn't disappear. It kept getting brighter and brighter, closer and closer.

"You're doing great, Michael. That's a fire up ahead. Just a few more steps."

Michael tried to stop. "No!" he said, slobbering his words. "It's the poachers, the...poachers." He lurched backward.

"It's a chance we have to take," I said. "We'll try to steal their medicine kit."

But Michael slumped over, his full weight against me. I thought we had found the fire too late. Tears came into my eyes. "Hang in there, Michael," I whispered, my voice sobbing. "Just a little longer."

I was dragging him now, and we made our way closer to the fire. If it was the poachers, I'd have to steal the medicine kit right away. There was no time to waste.

But as we got to within about 20 feet of the fire, I smelled a familiar scent that I couldn't quite place—kind of sweet, like honey, or maybe licorice. I thought I must be going crazy with worry and exhaustion.

Then I remembered. It was the smell of the Swamp Witch's tea! As we burst into the clearing around the fire, the witch was dancing around in its weird glow, singing a strange song. Blue, orange, and yellow flames leapt skyward. Sparks of purple light flashed from her fingers.

I knew I must be hallucinating. "Roselyn!" I called. "Help us!"

Michael and I collapsed to the ground together and I blacked out.

CHAPTER 9
Alligator Food

TEETH! All I could see were teeth. The alligator's huge, gaping mouth snapped open and shut only inches from my face.

I thrashed around, trying to escape the powerful, invisible bonds that held me. Closer and closer came the monstrous creature, until I thought it would get me for sure.

Then, out of the mists, I saw the Swamp Witch. She stood over Michael's lifeless body, her hands raised, her voice chanting eerie spells. On the fire was a black kettle. She danced a weird step as she added ingredients to the hissing brew. Then, with a cackle, she dipped a huge spoon into the pot and brought up a steaming, spitting scoop of wiggling snakes, lizards, and creatures I couldn't even recognize.

She held out the spoon to Michael, who was standing now, swaying in front of her as if he was in a trance. My horrified eyes saw a freshly dug grave behind him, black and wide. He was just about to take a sip, when I finally forced myself to wake up.

"NO!" I screamed as I jerked myself upright. "Don't drink that! It's poison!" I lunged toward him.

"What are you talking about, Ryan?" Michael asked in a normal voice.

I shook my head and rubbed my eyes.

"W-w-what is this? You're all right?"

"Yeah, I feel a lot better. Roselyn fixed me up with some Indian medicines and this mud pack."

Michael was sitting on his sleeping bag next to the small fire. He had a tin cup in one hand and a plate of biscuits and scrambled eggs in his lap. His other hand, the one with the snakebite, was covered with a thick layer of mud and herbs.

"I...I must have been having a nightmare," I said. "It seemed so real though. Are we really here? Are we really okay?"

"Yeah, you've been thrashing around all morning. And yeah, I think we're okay," Michael said.

I got up and walked over to the fire to sit next to him. "That stuff on your hand smells disgusting," I said.

"I don't know what it is," he answered. "Roselyn crushed it to draw the poison out."

"Where's the Swamp Witch now?" I asked.

"Out scouting," he answered.

"Where are we?" I asked.

"Doesn't this place look familiar?"

I looked around and realized that we were back under the thatched shelter from the night before. "We must have gone in a big circle," I said.

"Yeah, I guess we did," Michael said.

Michael must have read my mind, because he said, "She wouldn't fix me up so she could leave us alone to die. She'll be back, don't worry. And she's not a witch, remember? She's a scientist."

I got myself some eggs and a biscuit. It was, without a doubt, the best food I'd ever tasted in my life. I started to feel better after about three helpings. "Hey, what's that?" I asked.

Michael handed the object to me. "Neat, huh?"

I stared at the thing. Gleaming white, polished from years in the sun, the single bone with at least 20 perfectly preserved teeth brought back all the feelings of my nightmare about the alligator.

"This is the jawbone of an alligator," I said. "Where'd you get this?"

"Roselyn gave it to me for good luck and to ward off evil spirits."

"She sounds like a witch to me," I said.

"She wasn't serious. She just said it might come in handy someday, that's all," Michael said. "All I know is that she got the snake poison out of me and I'm fine now. I don't care if she *is* a witch, she saved my life, didn't she?"

"Don't you boys have anything better to do than tell witch stories?"

I heard Roselyn's voice as she came up behind us.

"I've got something better for us to do," she added. "I found the poachers and Rick. We don't have much time. I heard them say they were leaving today."

We were so glad to see her that we forgot to ask her where she'd been. "What are we waiting for?" I asked. "Let's go!"

Silently moving through the swamp, we made our way to where Roselyn had spotted the poachers.

"We could have walked this in an hour yesterday if we hadn't gotten lost," I whispered to Michael.

He nodded.

We stepped off the sandy soil and slid without a sound through the slime beneath the cypress trees. Very carefully, we poked our heads around one of the thick trunks. Roselyn stood between us.

In front of us was a scene that was even worse than my terrible nightmare. Rick was tied up against another cypress tree. His arms were bent way back. I winced when I thought about how much it must have hurt. His legs were tied so that he had to stand.

Dennis Griffin and the one-armed Mr. Smith from the airboat tour were standing on the other side of the camp in front of a bundle of bloody alligator skins. A small fiberglass raft filled with swimming alligator hatchlings stood a short distance away.

"So that's how they get them out of here," I whispered in Roselyn's ear. "They float them out in the raft."

"I think we should pack up and get ourselves out of here, Billy," Griffin was saying to the pirate, the one who had called himself Mr. Smith on the tour. "Thanks to the information we beat out of the teacher, we got enough gators to keep us going for awhile. And I don't trust those kids."

"I knew that guy's name wasn't Mr. Smith," I murmured.

"Those kids are probably dead by now," the pirate said. "And no one will come looking for them because they're scared to death by those stories you spread about the Swamp Witch, Roscoe," Billy said.

"I thought his name was Dennis Griffin," Michael whispered.

"Yeah, what a riot!" Roscoe said. "We sure freaked out that Griffin guy with our search lights and our ghostly voices in the swamp. He did us a real favor by going crazy and telling those stories about some stupid witch in here. That was just the smoke screen we needed to keep people from sticking their noses into our little business. Ha-ha!" He patted the ranger badge on his shirt. "Taking over Griffin's identity was a perfect cover!"

"The guy in the mental hospital must be the real Dennis Griffin," I said.

Billy, the pirate, stepped forward. "Don't forget, Mr. Smart Guy, you wouldn't have had no business if I hadn't paid attention on that airboat ride. That kid fooled you when he showed you all those phony spots on the map. But he led me right to the best spots."

"Oh no," I whispered. "We led them right to the gator holes!"

Roselyn patted me on the shoulder and said, "You didn't know. It's not your fault."

"I knew that guy was up to no good," Michael said. "He took too many notes and asked too many questions."

"Shh! Did you hear that?" Roscoe asked. He stared in our direction.

We hid behind the tree and waited a long time before we peeked around again. This time they were standing in front of Rick. Billy was waving his alligator skinning knife in front of Rick's face.

"All right, Teach," he bellowed. "We got time to grab us one more batch of gators before we meet the plane. Where are they?"

Rick shook his head. "You slimeballs can rot in the swamp for all I care. I'm not telling you another thing."

"So that's why they kidnapped Rick—so he could lead them to the gators!" I whispered to Michael.

"You want to be dead like those gators over there?" Billy hollered.

"You're going to kill me anyway, so what's the difference?" Rick asked.

"You'd die for a couple of lousy reptiles? You're even dumber than I thought," Roscoe yelled.

I made a move to help Rick, but Roselyn stopped me. "There's nothing we can do yet."

"What are we supposed to do? Just sit here and let them torture Rick?" I asked her.

Michael leaned in closer. "We'll have to catch them off guard," Roselyn said. "We'll try to separate them."

"But how?" Michael asked.

With our heads bent together whispering, we didn't notice how quiet the poachers had become until it was too late.

Suddenly, the ugly stump of Billy's arm was wrapped around my neck, his hook inches from my face. His other hand held my arm bent up against my back. He jerked it and I gasped in pain. Michael was pinned to the ground by Roscoe, his face smashed into the muck. He was twisting from side to side, trying to get a breath.

"Let him up. He can't breathe!" I said.

"Aww, poor thing," Roscoe said, grabbing Michael by the collar and lifting his face out of the water. I heard Michael suck in air before Roscoe shoved him down again.

They dragged us out of the swamp into the clearing where Rick was tied up.

"Looky here, Teach," Billy said. "We just found us some alligator food!"

The Swamp Witch had disappeared again. It was as if she could disappear into the air, whenever she wanted!

CHAPTER 10
Left to Rot

"TOES and fingers would be good for starters, don't you think so, Billy Boy?" Roscoe laughed.

"Yeah," he answered, "at least until the gators start growling for something more than just appetizers!"

The way they both laughed made me sick. They tied us to trees next to Rick. Then they left us alone while they cooked and ate alligator steaks.

"Are you all right?" I whispered to Rick. "Are you hurt?"

"I'm okay. How did you find me?"

"The Swamp Witch helped us," Michael answered. "We found her, just like you said."

Rick's eyes opened wide. "What?!?" he whispered. "You mean you really found her?"

I didn't understand. "Well, yeah. Isn't that what you wanted us to do?"

Rick shook his head. "I can't believe it! There's got to be some explanation. I left that note so you would know what part of the swamp these guys were taking me to—the Black Swamp, where she's supposed to live. I didn't really mean for you to find the Swamp Witch, or whoever this person is. I mean, the Swamp Witch is just a legend."

"She's not just a legend, Rick," I whispered. Then we told him all about her, how she saved Michael from the snakebite, how she lived in the hut, and how she was a scientist working for the Park Service.

"She said she knew you, Rick, or at least knew *about* you," said Michael.

I could tell Rick thought we had been wandering around the swamp too long. He finally just shook his head and said, "Well, however you got here, I wish things didn't look so bad."

"What's that, Teach?" shouted Billy. "Aren't your little friends enjoying their stay with us?" He got up and came over to us, carrying his knife. "Now, Teach, I think you were just about to tell us where we could find some more gators."

"Go ahead and kill me," Rick muttered. "I won't tell you anything."

Billy laughed. "I wouldn't dream of hurting

you any more. Oh no. It's your friend here I'm going to hurt!" He stared at Michael for a second. Then he knelt in front of Michael and pulled off Michael's boot. He clamped Michael's toe in his hook and held the knife right above it.

"Talk, Teach. You've got 10 seconds before it's time to feed the gators." Billy looked back and forth between Michael and Rick.

"No, you can't!" I yelled.

"One, two, three..." he counted.

"You're bluffing," Rick said.

"Four, five, six..."

Roscoe stirred the water in the alligator-filled raft with a stick. "Count faster, Billy, these critters are getting hungry," he said.

"Seven, eight, nine..."

"NOOO!" Michael screamed.

"All right, you win," said Rick. "I can't let you hurt him. I'll tell you what you want to know." Michael and I breathed a huge sigh of relief as Billy released his foot.

Where was Roselyn? She always seemed to disappear when the going got tough. It's the understatement of the year to say we needed her help!

"You'll find a large colony of alligators in Langtry Prairie, in the northwest corner along the sandy bank of the Lasso river."

I looked at Rick and understood what he was doing. The alligator colony at Langtry had cleared out years ago.

"Come on, Roscoe. Let's pack this stuff on out of here and pick up a few more skins on the way. We have to meet the seaplane at dawn tomorrow. Cut the teacher loose. We'll take him with us for insurance."

"All the way to Mexico?" asked Roscoe.

"Nah," Billy answered with that obnoxious laugh of his. "Let's take him about halfway across the Gulf. He can swim the rest of the way. Ha-ha!"

"What about the boy scouts?" Roscoe asked with a sneer. Billy walked over to us. "They just got here," he said. "It would be a shame if they didn't have a chance to have a look around. Let's just leave them here.

"Good idea," added Roscoe. "If the alligators don't get them, the snakes will. And even if they do get out, they'll be as loony as that ranger fellow."

"Yeah," said Billy with another laugh. "Watch out for the Swamp Witch, boys. Don't let her try to eat you!"

Still laughing their heads off, the men lifted their packs. Roscoe carried the skins with a big leather strap. Billy hooked a wide belt around Rick's waist and onto the two rope loops on the raft.

Just before they left, Roscoe came over to check our ropes. He pulled mine tighter. I yelped with pain. It felt like my arms were going to pop out of my shoulders. Michael's face was still covered with swamp mud. His legs jerked. He looked pathetic.

As Roscoe walked toward him, Michael fainted. His eyes rolled back and his head flopped to the side.

"Forget him," Billy ordered from the trees. "Let's get going."

Roscoe gave Michael's head a shove and it flopped to the other side. Michael drooled.

"Pull!" Billy ordered, as if Rick was a donkey. In a few minutes, they were headed out, with Billy poking Rick with a stick.

I was worried about Michael. It looked like the snake poison was finally getting to him and causing convulsions. As the poachers crashed off through the trees, I stuck my toe out as far as I could and nudged Michael's foot.

"Michael, wake up! Are you okay?"

I saw his arm moving. Slowly, his muscles flexed and relaxed. Suddenly his head snapped up and he smiled through the muck on his face. In a second his arms were free!

"Ta da!" he exclaimed. In his hand he was

holding the alligator jawbone that the witch had given him for good luck.

"How long have you been working on that?" I asked as Michael crawled over to untie me.

"Ever since we got here. It's not as good as a saw or a knife, but it worked," he said.

He sawed away on my ropes with the bone. In a few minutes, my arms dropped down and the feeling started tingling back into them. Then he freed my legs.

"I thought we were goners," I said.

"You know it," he agreed. "I've really gotten attached to my big toe. I don't know what I'd do without it."

"Skateboarding would be pretty tough with only nine toes, wouldn't it?"

"I don't know. I've never tried it," he said as we walked down to the water to wash off.

"Hey, that fainting act of yours was great," I said as Michael leaned over the water and rinsed the muck off his face and hair. "It looks like you've had a lot of practice drooling. You deserve an award..."

My words died in mid-sentence.

"Michael! Watch out!"

CHAPTER 11
Too Close for Comfort

I saw the periscope eyes and snout of a large, adult alligator zooming silently through the water, directly toward Michael. The water barely rippled as the gator dove for its final lunge.

I sailed through the air and knocked Michael out of the way, just as the alligator lunged out of the water at him. The huge jaws snapped shut, snatching only air. We scrambled up the bank as the alligator slid back into the water.

"Whew! I thought alligators didn't usually attack people," Michael said, trembling. "That's twice since I've been here."

"He smells death at this place," I said, looking around at the blood-soaked rocks, the cooked alligator meat at the campfire, and the pile of dead baby gators.

"Let's get out of here before anything else

happens," Michael urged.

"The poachers' trail should be easy to follow, with Rick dragging that raft filled with alligators."

"Yeah," Michael added. "We have to stop them before the plane takes off at dawn tomorrow. We shouldn't have any trouble catching up with them."

That was true. Wherever they had gone, the grass was all flattened from dragging the raft. We walked along, but we didn't talk much. Each of us had our own thoughts. I kept thinking about how close we had come to being killed. Those poachers had actually left us there to die. If it wasn't for the jawbone that Roselyn had given Michael, it would probably have been all over for us. That reminded me.

"Where do you think Roselyn went?"

"I don't know," Michael answered. "I hope she's around, though. We're going to need her help."

"That's for sure."

We followed the poachers' trail as the sun started to go down. We couldn't stop to rest for long because we didn't want to risk missing the plane at dawn. Luckily, because the raft they were dragging was so big, it wasn't hard to follow the trail, even in the dark.

When we stopped to rest at about midnight, Michael said in a low voice, "Do you see it? Over there?" He pointed off into the swamp. About 75 yards or so away, I thought I could just make out a faint glow.

"I thought I had seen it a couple times earlier," Michael explained. "Now I'm sure it's a light of some kind."

He looked at me, and I knew we were both thinking the same thing. "Do you think..."

"It might be her. Or it might be swamp gases, or lightning bugs," Michael said.

We saw the glow a few more times, but it never came close enough so we could be sure what it was. As it was getting close to dawn, we started to walk as quietly as we could. I knew we were getting close. The poachers couldn't be more than a quarter-mile in front of us. It was about time for the final confrontation. I only wished we were sure we would have Roselyn's help.

Suddenly, a motor roared to life not more than a hundred yards in front of us. We broke into a run.

We burst out of the pine forest into an open meadow of waving grass. The Park Service's airboat, the one that Roscoe had stolen when he was pretending to be Dennis Griffin, was stopped on the edge of the water. Then we saw them, loading the skins into a seaplane.

"Roselyn said we had to catch them in the act and hold them until the authorities arrived. We can't let that plane take off!" I said.

"But how are we going to stop it?" Michael asked in desperation.

By this time the cargo was loaded onto the plane and we could see Roscoe and Billy shoving Rick into the cockpit of the seaplane.

"Into the airboat!" I said as their plane began to rev its motor. We leaped into the airboat and I started the engine. Their seaplane started to taxi across the grass on its pontoon landing gear.

I slammed the boat into gear and we raced after the plane. "The radio should be in that box under the seat," I shouted above the sound of the boat engine. "Call for help. Tell them we're at Langtry Prairie on the edge of Pirate's Lagoon."

Michael radioed for help. I revved the engine up to full power. The propeller case shook with the force of the wind. I thought the airboat might explode, but we were gaining on them. We had almost caught up with the plane before they saw us.

Michael gave me a thumbs-up. "They're coming," he yelled.

"They see us!" I shouted. "Get down!"

The seaplane turned and came back toward us. We heard the crack of gunshots, and bullets whizzed over us.

"To the left," Michael yelled. "Now, to the right. Keep them guessing."

I swerved hard to the right, then reversed and spun the boat around 180 degrees. We headed away from them, back toward the swamp, leading them on a wild chase around the meadow. All the time, shots kept hitting the water around us. One bullet zinged off the front railing of the boat.

After they had chased us for a while, it looked like they decided to forget about us and take off.

"Where's that helicopter?" I asked. "I thought you said it was coming!"

Michael shrugged.

"We can't lose them now," I yelled. I swung the airboat in a wide arc and took off after the plane. I had the angle on them, so I was trying to cut them off before they could get into the air.

"Get some thick rope out of the tackle box," I said. "I'm going to swing around in front of the plane. You throw the rope into the propeller."

"You're crazy!" Michael yelled.

"Well, if you want, you can reach up and

just grab the propeller!" I said sarcastically.

"I'll toss the rope. Just get me close," he said.

"Don't worry, we'll be close—too close for comfort!"

I pushed the boat to full throttle and aimed right across the oncoming path of the seaplane. *Either we make it or we go up in flames,* I thought.

We closed the gap on the plane. As we headed toward a collision, I could see Roscoe's face staring out at us, filled with hatred. But I couldn't see Rick.

In another few seconds, we were almost to the seaplane. A bullet from the open cabin window whizzed by my shoulder. Just as we reached it, the plane started to lift off the water with a tremendous roar.

"Hurry! Throw that rope!"

For a second I was sure the plane was going to hit us. But it rose up and I could feel the heat of the plane's engine as it passed over us.

Michael stood up and tossed the rope into the propeller. He ducked just in time. The propeller choked and sputtered and made an awful noise. Pieces of chewed up rope flew through the air. The pilot swerved to avoid us, but he had no power. Seconds later, the seaplane crashed into a stand of mangrove trees on the water's edge.

Then we saw the helicopter zooming in over the trees on the other side of the lagoon, heading our way. We headed over to where the plane was. Roscoe and Billy had stumbled out, and were aiming their guns at us.

"Blow them away!" Roscoe roared. "We should have killed them back in the swamp!"

We were sitting ducks. But just as he and Billy were taking aim at us, the swamp in front of them exploded in fire and purple smoke. It was like the Fourth of July, with sparks, flames, smoke, and loud bangs everywhere!

The poachers screamed and dropped their guns. They covered their eyes.

"I can't see! There's something in my eyes!" Billy shouted.

"Aiiee! I'm blind!" screamed Roscoe.

We looked around, hardly believing we were safe. Then suddenly, above the roar of the approaching helicopter, we heard a sound I'll never forget as long as I live.

"Ah-ha-ah-ha-ha-ha-ha-ha-ha!"

It was the cackle of the Swamp Witch.

But we couldn't see her anywhere.

The helicopter landed next to the wreck and several armed park rangers were handcuffing Roscoe, Billy, and the pilot. They still couldn't see. Then Rick appeared in the doorway of the plane. We floated over to the downed plane and he crawled into the airboat.

"Incredible! You boys saved my life," he said, looking pretty shaky.

"I think we had a lot of help," I said with a glance at Michael.

"But where did you get those fireworks that you threw at the poachers? That was a great idea," said Rick.

"It wasn't us. It was the Swamp Witch!" Michael explained.

"Come on, guys, don't try to feed me that. You're heroes, take the credit you deserve," Rick said. "She's not real. She's just a story, a legend."

"But..."

We were interrupted by the approach of another airboat roaring into the lagoon.

"Look! It's Mom and Dad!" I shouted.

We ran over to tell them everything that had happened. Several park rangers took notes on what we said, while a couple others loaded the poachers into the helicopter. The last I saw of them was Billy's ugly hook, tied behind his back, as he was pushed aboard.

It took a long time to tell the whole story. The rangers wrote down what we said about Roselyn, but I could see them giving each other funny looks. Even Mom and Dad looked concerned, like they thought we had been out in the swamp for too long. Maybe they were thinking we'd have to join the real Dennis Griffin in the mental hospital.

"Then the Swamp Wi..., I mean Roselyn, threw fireworks at the poachers, something got in their eyes, and they dropped their guns, and you guys caught them. That's it," I explained.

After a moment of silence, in which the adults all looked serious, as if they really thought the strain of being in the swamp had been too much for us, Rick said, "Well, tell me how you got loose from the ropes so fast."

"Roselyn gave me this alligator jawbone for good luck," Michael said, reaching into his jeans pocket. "I used it to cut through...hey, where is it?"

"It's not there?" I said.

"No," Michael said sadly. "Shoot, I really wanted to keep it for a souvenir."

"It must have fallen out sometime on the trip or on the chase," I said.

"Well, never mind," said Mom, "I think it's time we all went home. I think you boys could use a good long rest. You're safe now, so let's not talk about witches or poachers or anything like that."

CHAPTER 12
Return to Roselyn's

AFTER a week of rest, we were back over at Rick's house to take the camping trip that we never got to take.

"I don't think I'll have to teach you guys survival skills," Rick said. "How about a little plant and animal identification? We can make some plaster casts of footprints and things like that."

"That sounds tame enough," I told him. "That's about my speed after what we've been through."

Then I looked at Michael. "Hey, Rick," he said. "There's something we want to ask you. We're going to be in the same area where Roselyn's chickee hut is. We were wondering if we could stop there and just say thanks for everything. She did save my life, you know."

"And yours and mine, Rick," I added.

Rick shook his head, like he was wondering what to say. After all of the adults seemed to think that we had just imagined the Swamp Witch stuff, Michael and I had stopped talking about it, except to each other.

"Guys, I already told you. The Park Service says it doesn't have a scientist named Roselyn living out in the swamp."

"Well, maybe they know her by another name, or maybe she works for someone else. We can't remember exactly," said Michael.

"Please, Rick, it's right on the way," I pleaded.

"Besides," added Michael, "if we go, then we can find out once and for all if she really exists."

Rick sighed. "Okay, I guess there's no harm."

*   *   *   *   *

"There!" I shouted and pointed ahead. "That's where we beached the dugout canoe. We followed the path up there."

I led the way. First we passed through the small clearing where Michael and I had slept that first night.

"Is this the place?" Michael asked. "Where's our fire ring?"

"I think this is the place," I told him.

"Maybe the rain washed away the fire ring."

But the closer we got to Roselyn's hut, the stranger I began to feel. It was almost like the swamp had covered all the evidence that we had ever been there. It felt as if we were walking into the past. The path felt strange and familiar at the same time, like something you've seen in a dream.

But then Michael cried out and pointed up ahead. There, hanging from the tree, was Harry, good old Harry. I've never been so happy to see a skeleton! That proved we had been there after all!

"There it is!" Michael said, pointing through the trees. "I'm going to ask her for another alligator jawbone to replace the one I lost in the rescue."

We ran ahead, with Rick behind, and came into the clearing where the hut stood.

"Hey, Roselyn. Hi!" we called. I knocked on the door, expecting her familiar voice to answer. The door swung open at my touch.

"No!" I cried. "I don't believe it."

Michael ran up to my side. "What's wrong?"

Without a word, I brushed aside the thick, dusty cobwebs and walked into the hut. Michael and Rick followed.

I pulled my flashlight from my pack and swung the beam around the room. Everything was buried by dust and cobwebs. The iron stove was cold and rusty. Where Roselyn's shelves of specimen jars had been, there was only dirt and leaves. Her heavy, black pot stood in the corner with weeds growing out of the cracks.

"I-I-I can't believe it!" I stuttered.

"We were here just a week ago. The place was spotless," Michael exclaimed. "She cooked us rabbit stew in that pot. She lit oil lamps. She showed us her barrels full of rainwater and her journals full of wildlife notes."

Rick walked around the deserted room. "I don't think anyone's lived here for years."

"But we were here, I know we were. She helped us," Michael said.

"Look around," Rick said. "What do your eyes tell you? I'm looking at it like a scientist. No one's been here for years!"

"But... it all seemed so real," I said. I felt like I was close to crying. "I-I don't know what to think anymore," I confessed. "How could Roselyn not be real?"

"How could she be real?" Rick said softly. "Deep down, you know there's no such thing as a Swamp Witch. You could have imagined the whole thing, with all the stress and danger you were in."

I just shrugged. I had wanted to believe

that she was real. Now, I just didn't know.

Rick went on. "Look, I'm not saying you guys made it all up. I think that our minds can play some pretty strange tricks on us sometimes. You know I'm a scientist. That's the way I have to look at things. There's got to be an explanation for everything."

Michael had been quiet while Rick and I were talking. Suddenly he spoke. The tone of his voice was weird, almost unearthly.

"You say you have to look at things like a scientist, Rick," Michael said, barely louder than a whisper.

"That's right," Rick answered.

"Then tell me how you look at this. I found it on the table."

Michael held out his hand. In it, so smooth and shiny and white that it seemed to glow in the darkened room, was the alligator jawbone.

About the Author

Always an adventurer at heart, backpacking and wilderness camping are among C.K.'s favorite hobbies. As a child, C.K. used to spend hours in the wild, overgrown forests of southern Florida, blazing trails, collecting insects, and making Indian huts and ovens out of mud and sticks.

"I've always felt very close to life in the Everglades," says C.K. "Some of my fondest memories are of trips there with my parents. The atmosphere is so special, so full of excitement. You never know what may be hiding around the next bend—maybe even an alligator. And if you get separated from your group, the quiet closes in around you. Then it feels as if you are the only person left in the world!"